STARS OF MINE

Stars of Mine

Kevin Crossley-Holland

With illustrations by
Martina Peluso

First published in 2013 in Great Britain by
Barrington Stoke Ltd
18 Walker Street, Edinburgh, EH3 7LP

www.barringtonstoke.co.uk

This story was first published in a different form in
The Old Stories published by Orion Children's Books, 1999

ISBN: 978-1-78112-192-4

Printed in China by Leo

This book has dyslexia-friendly features

For Jessica – with love

Contents

Chapter 1

There was once a little old cottage where a mother lived with her giddy girl. The girl was just sixteen, and as sweet as honey.

One fine day, the mother made five meat pies and put them in the oven. But then the woman from next door called round.

They were soon so busy with gossip that the mother forgot about the pies. By the time she took them out of the oven, their crusts were as hard as the bark of an old oak tree.

"Girl," she said, "you put them there pies in the larder."

"My! I'm that hungry," said the girl.

"Leave them there and they'll come again," said the mother. That was an old saying. It meant that the crusts would get soft when the pies had cooled down.

But the girl didn't know that. "Well!" she said to herself. "If the pies will come again, I'll eat these ones now." And so she set to work and ate them all, every bite.

When it was supper time, the mother felt very hungry.

"I could just do with one of them there pies," she said to the girl. "Go and get one off the shelf. They'll have come again by now."

The girl went and looked. There was nothing on the shelf but an empty dish.

"No!" she called. "They haven't come again."

"Not none of them?" said the mother.

"No!" called the girl. "Not none."

"Well!" said her mother. "Come again or not, I'll have one for my supper."

"You can't if they haven't come again," said the girl. "I've eaten the lot. You can't have one until it's come again."

Her mother was very angry. "You've eaten the lot?" she shouted. "You greedyguts!"

Chapter 2

The mother carried her spinning wheel over to the door. She was still angry. To calm herself, she began to spin. As she spun she sang.

"My girl ate five, five pies today. My girl ate five, five pies today."

The king came down the street and heard the woman.

"What were those words, woman?" he said. "What were you singing?"

The mother felt ashamed of her daughter's greed. "Well!" she said, and began to spin again:

"My girl spun five,

five sacks of wool today.

My girl spun five sacks today."

"Stars of mine!" said the king. "I never heard of anyone who could do that."

The king raised his eyes and looked at the girl, so sweet and giddy and sixteen.

"Five today," said the woman. "Five sacks full."

"Look here!" said the king. "I want a wife and I'll marry your girl. For eleven months of the year she can eat as much

food as she likes. She can buy all the

dresses she wants. She can have all the

friends and music she wishes. But when

the last month of the year comes, she'll

have to spin five sacks of wool every day.

If she doesn't, I'll cut off her head."

"All right!" said the mother. "That's all right, isn't it, girl?"

The woman was pleased as pleased at the thought that her girl was going to marry the king. She wasn't worried about the five sacks of wool.

"When that comes to it," she said to the girl later, "we'll find a way out of it. But I reckon he'll have clean forgotten about it."

Chapter 3

So the king and the girl were married. For eleven months the girl ate as much food as she liked. She bought all the dresses she wanted. She had all the friends and music she wished.

As the last month of the eleven passed, the girl began to think about those sacks of wool. She wondered if the king was thinking about them too. But the king said not a word, and the girl was quite sure that he had forgotten them.

But on the very last day of the month, the king led the girl up to a room in the palace she had never set eyes on

before. There was nothing in it but a
spinning wheel and a stool.

"Now, my dear," said the king, "you'll be shut in here tomorrow with some food and five sacks of wool. And if you haven't spun all five sacks before dark, your head will be cut off."

Then away went the king to do the things a king has to do.

Well, the girl was that scared! She had always been such a giddy girl, and she didn't know how to spin. She didn't know what to do next morning, with no

one beside her and no one to help her.
She sat down on a stool in the palace
kitchen and heavens! How she did cry.

Chapter 4

All of a sudden, the girl heard a sort of knock low down on the door. She stood up and opened it, and what did she see but a small little black thing with a long tail. The small black thing looked up at her, all wide eyed. "What are you crying for?" it said.

"What's that to you?" said the girl.

"Never you mind," the black thing said. "Tell me what you're crying for."

"It won't do me no good if I do," the girl replied.

"You don't know that," the black thing said, and it twirled its tail round.

"Well!" said the girl. "If it don't do me no good, perhaps that won't do me no harm." So she told him about the pies and the spinning and everything.

"This is what I'll do," said the little black thing. "I'll come to your window every morning and take the wool, and I'll bring it back all spun before dark."

"What will that cost?" the girl asked.

The thing looked out of the corners of its eyes and it said, "Every night I'll give you three guesses at my name.

And if you haven't guessed it before the month's up, you shall be mine."

The girl thought she was bound to guess its name before the month was out. "All right!" she said. "I agree to that."

"All right!" that the black thing said, and lork – how it twirled its tail!

Chapter 5

The next morning, the king led the girl up to the room. The sacks of wool and the day's food were all ready for her.

"Now there's the wool," said the king. "And if it isn't spun before dark, off

goes your head!" Then he went out and locked the door.

As soon as the king had gone there was a knock at the window.

The girl stood up and opened the window and there was the little old thing sitting on the ledge.

"Where's the wool?" it said.

"Here you are!" she said. And she gave it the wool.

When it was early evening, there was a knock again at the window. The girl stood up and opened it. There was the little old thing, with a pile of fine, spun wool over its arm.

"Here you are!" it said, and it gave the flax to her. "And now," it said, "what's my name?"

"Is it Bill?" the girl said.

"No!" the thing said, "it ain't!" And it twirled its tail.

"Is it Ned?" the girl said.

"No!" the thing said, "it ain't!" And it twirled its tail.

"Well, is it Mark?" she said .

"No!" it said, "it ain't!" And it twirled its tail faster, and away it flew.

When the girl's husband came in, the five sacks of wool were ready for him.

"I'm glad I won't have to kill you tonight, my dear," he said. "You'll have more food and wool in the morning," he said.

And away he went again to do all the things a king has to do.

Well, the wool and the food were made ready for the girl each day, and each day the little black imp came in the morning and returned in the evening. And each day and all day the girl sat thinking of names to try out on the imp when it came back. But she never hit on the right one!

As days went on, the imp looked wickeder and wickeder. It twirled its tail faster and faster each time she made a guess.

Chapter 6

So they came to the last day of the month but one. The imp returned in the evening with the wool. "Ain't you guessed my name yet?" it said.

"Is it Barnabas?" the girl said.

"No! It aint," the imp said.

"Is it Samuel?" she said.

"No! It aint," it said.

"Ah well! Is it Zamzummims?" said she.

"No! It ain't that either," it said. And then it looked at the girl with eyes like burning coals.

"Woman," it said, "there's only tomorrow evening, and then you'll be mine!" And away it flew!

Well, the girl felt so afraid!

Soon she heard the king coming along the passage. When he had walked into the room and seen the wool, he said, "Well, my dear! As far as I can see, you'll have your wool spun tomorrow too. I reckon I won't have to kill you, so I'll have my supper in here tonight with you." Then the king's servants came with his supper, and another stool for him, and the two of them sat down together.

The king had only eaten a couple
of bites when he pushed back his stool,
waved his knife and fork, and began to
laugh.

"What is it?" asked the girl.

"I'll tell you," said the king. "I was
out hunting today, and I got lost. I came
to a place in the forest that I'd never
seen before. There was an old pit there.
And I heard a sort of humming. So I got

off my horse and crept up to the edge
of the pit and looked down. And do you
know what I saw? The oddest little black
imp you ever set eyes on! And what did
it have but a little spinning wheel?

It was spinning and spinning, faster than you could believe. It spun, and it twirled its tail, and as it spun, it sang.

"Nimmy nimmy not,

My name's Tom Tit Tot."

When the girl heard this, she felt as if she could have jumped out of her skin for joy. But she didn't say a word.

Chapter 7

Next morning, the small little black thing looked as wicked as wicked when it came for the wool. Just before it grew dark, she heard it knock at the window again. She opened the window and it came right in on to the sill. It was grinning from ear to ear, and ooh! Its tail was twirling round so fast.

"What's my name?" it said, as it gave her the spun wool.

"Is it Solomon?" she said, and she pretended to be afraid.

"Well, is it Zebedee?" she said again

"No, it ain't," said the imp. And then it laughed and twirled its tail so fast you could hardly see it.

"Take your time, woman," it said. "Next guess, and you're mine." And it stretched out its black hands towards her.

The girl backed away a step or two. She looked at it, and then she laughed and pointed a finger at it and sang out:

"**Nimmy nimmy not,**
Your name's Tom Tit Tot."

Well! When the imp heard her, it gave an awful shriek and away it flew into the dark. She never saw it again.

Chapter 8

So that was the end of Tom Tit Tot. For eleven more months the girl ate as much food as she liked. She bought all the dresses she wanted. She had all the friends and music she wished.

And then her husband said to her, "Well, my dear, that's been eleven months. Tomorrow you'll have to begin again, and spin your five sacks of wool every day."

The girl reckoned her husband had clean forgotten about the wool, and now she didn't know what to do. She couldn't count on Tom Tit Tot again, and she couldn't spin a mite herself. Her head would have to come off!

Poor girl! She sat down on a stool in the kitchen, and she cried as if her heart would break.

All at once, the girl heard a knock at
the door. So she got up and unlocked it.
There stood a gipsy woman, as brown as
a berry.

"Well, well! What's all this to-do?" the gipsy woman said. "What are you crying like that for?"

"Get away, you gipsy woman," said the girl. "Don't you poke your nose in where it's no use."

"Tell me what's wrong, and maybe I *shall* be some use," said the woman. And she looked so kind that the girl told her.

"Is that all?" the woman said. "I've helped people out of worse holes than that. Now I'll help you."

"Ah! But what will you ask for helping me?" said the girl. She was thinking of how she'd almost given herself away to the wicked little black imp.

"I don't want anything but the best
suit of clothes you've got," said the gipsy.

"You shall have them, and welcome," said the girl. She ran and opened the chest where her best dresses and things were. She gave a fine dress to the woman, and a ring of yellow gold.

"Well," the girl said to herself, "if she's a cheat and she can't help me, then my head will be cut off. So it won't matter anyhow if I've given away my best gown."

The woman was thrilled when she saw the gown. "Now then!" she said. "You'll have to ask all the people you know to a fine party, and I'll come to it too. Then your problems will all be over."

Chapter 9

The girl went to her husband. "My dear," she said, "seeing as this is the last night before I go away to spin, I should like to have a party."

"All right, my dear," said the king.

So the people were all asked, and
they came in their best clothes. There
were silks and satins, and all manner
of fine things. They had a grand supper
with the best of foods, and they enjoyed

themselves a great deal. But the gipsy woman never came near the place.

The girl's heart was in her mouth with fear.

One of the lords grew tired of dancing. He said it wasn't long till midnight, and it was time to go.

"No, no! Stay a little longer," said the girl. "Let's have a game of blind man's bluff before you go." So they began to play.

Just then the door flew open, and in came the gipsy woman. She'd washed herself, and brushed her hair, and wound satin round her head. With the grand gown, she looked like a queen.

"Stars of mine!" said the king. "Who's that?"

"Oh! She's one of my friends," said the girl. And she watched to see what the gipsy would do.

"Are you playing blind man's bluff?" said the gipsy. "I'll join in with you."

And so she did. But what was in her pocket but a little pot of black oil?

As she ran around, she dipped her hand in this oil, and smeared it on people as she brushed past.

It wasn't long before someone cried out. "Oh lord! There's some nasty stuff on my gown."

"Why, it's on my dress too," said another. "That must have come off you."

"No! It didn't! You've put it on me."

And then everyone began to shout and quarrel. The ladies cried, and the gentlemen shouted, and all their fine clothes were smeared with oil.

Chapter 10

The king stepped forward. "Why, what's this?" he said. There was a great mark on the sleeve of his coat. He smelt it and turned up his nose. "That's oil from a cart," he said.

"No, it isn't," said the gipsy woman. "That came off my hand. It's grease from my spinning wheel.

You see," she said, "I'm a great spinner. I spun and I spun and I spun. I got so good that I could spin five sacks of wool in one day. And because I spun so much, the oil worked into my hands."

The gipsy waved her hands above her head.

"Now it doesn't matter how often I wash them," she said. "They still won't come clean. I dirty everything I touch. I hope your wife doesn't spin as much as I do. If she does, the oil will get into her hands just like mine."

"The king looked at his coat, and he rubbed it and sniffed at it and then he looked at his wife. "Look here, my dear," he said, "and listen to what I say. If I see you sit down at a spinning wheel one more time, your head will come off!"

So the girl never had to spin again.

And that's all!

Our books are tested
for children and young people by
children and young people.

Thanks to everyone who consulted on
a manuscript for their time and effort in
helping us to make our books better
for our readers.